THE ALPHABET SOUP

by MIRKO GABLER

Henry Holt and Company

New York

For Ann, Alec, and Luke
—M. G.

First edition
Published by Henry Holt and Company, Inc., 115 West 18th Street,
New York, New York 10011.
Published simultaneously in Canada by Fitzhenry & Whiteside
Ltd., 91 Granton Drive, Richmond Hill, Ontario L4B 2N5.

Library of Congress Cataloging-in-Publication Data
Gabler, Mirko.
   The alphabet soup / by Mirko Gabler.
   Summary: When he follows the witch twins Gurgla and Blog
home from school, Zack almost becomes the final ingredient in
their alphabet soup.
   ISBN 0-8050-2049-7
   [1. Witches—Fiction.   2. Alphabet—Fiction.]   I. Title.
PZ7.G1154A1   1992
[E]—dc20   92-1127

Printed in the United States of America on acid-free paper. ∞

10   9   8   7   6   5   4   3   2   1

Gurgla and Blog were twins. They lived deep in the woods with an old witch, who also happened to be their mother. One day the witch decided that it was time for the youngsters to learn to read, and she sent them off to school in the village. Miss Smith, their new teacher, introduced the twins to her class and then cut their enormous fingernails so that they could hold their pencils better. The twins liked school very much, and by the end of the day, they already knew the alphabet. Their first homework assignment was to make a bowl of alphabet soup.

They ran home singing. "ABCDEFG…HIJKLMNOP…QRS…TUV…"
Once in a while they would stop to swallow a slug or a snail, for
they had forgotten to bring a lunch, and now they were very hungry.

"W…XYZ, now we know our ABCs, la la la" and on and on.

They had no idea that one of their classmates, a curious boy named
Zack, was following them home.

Their home stood in the middle of a swamp on two chicken legs. On the roof, like a wild hairdo, grew a mountain of weeds. Gurgla and Blog threw a rock at the cottage door.

"We're home, Mother!" they cried. Zack jumped behind a poisonberry bush.

The creaky door opened. An ugly witch stuck her head out.

"Mom," squealed Gurgla, "we want to make some alphabet soup!" And Blog added in his deep voice, "It's our homework!"

"What?" she croaked. "Alphabet soup? What kind of nonsense is that?"

"You'll see," said Gurgla. "Just get the cauldron ready!"

The twins rolled up their sleeves and chopped lots of firewood. Their mother started a fire, and soon the water in the cauldron was boiling.

"We'll start with the letter A!" said Gurgla, and indeed they did.

"A!" called Gurgla.

"ANTS," answered Blog, scooping a handful of carpenter ants out of a dead tree and dropping them in. The old witch stirred the pot, and they were ready for the letter B.

"B!"

"BAGWORM!" shouted Blog. He loved bagworms in his soup and knew where to find them. The old witch was pleased that her children were taking an interest in cooking.

The cauldron bubbled furiously, and Zack wondered if they might put in celery for C. But the twins didn't care for vegetables, and when Gurgla called "C!" Blog brought out a bucketful of CRUNCHY CRABS and dumped them into the pot.

The steam from the cauldron swirled around Gurgla's nose. She took a sniff, found the aroma delicious, and announced the next letter.

"D!"

"DANDRUFF! DUSTY DIRTY DANDRUFF!" blurted the witch.

"Well done, Mom," said Gurgla, and they all brushed their greasy hair onto a piece of newspaper, crumpled it up, and threw it in.

Zack's stomach was beginning to feel pretty queasy, but he decided that no matter what, he would stay until the soup was done. Will they really eat it? he wondered.

"E!" continued Gurgla.

"EAR!" shouted Blog. He took out his pocketknife and looked at Gurgla, who had the biggest ears in the family.

"Don't you dare!" Gurgla screeched. Blog, of course, was only kidding.

"How about an EARWIG!" suggested their mother. A whole flock of earwigs lived between her toes, and *splash!* into the pot they went. Now the old witch dipped her finger in to have a taste. Gurgla cried out with disgust.

"Yuck! She put a finger in our soup!"

The witch reached into her apron. "It needs some pepper."

"But Mom," said Blog, "pepper begins with P! Don't put it in yet; you'll spoil our soup!"

After some squabbling, Gurgla announced the letter F.

"FLAT FRIED FROG!" offered Blog proudly, and it just so happened that their mother had one in a jar. Gurgla was getting very hungry.

For the letter G, Gurgla added her mother's GALOSHES. The soup was getting thicker now, and it was beginning to stink.

Gurgla and Blog argued about who would lick the stick. Their empty stomachs growled.

"Stop fooling around!" cried the witch. Now she was hungry too. She took charge of the cooking.

"Well," she snapped, "what's next?"

"H!" squeaked Gurgla.

"HAT!" said the witch, and tossed her old hat into the pot. She was glad to get rid of it. It was full of holes anyway, and the bats were moving in.

"I!"

"INK!"

"J!"

"JELLYFISH JERKY!"

And so it went, like clockwork.

The cauldron was filling up fast.
"K!"
"KIPPERS!"
"L!"
"LUMPY LIVERWURST!"
"M!"
"MIGHTY MOLDY MUSHROOMS!"
"N!"
"NINCOMPOOP!"
"N!"

"Nincompoop! Nincompoop?" There was no nincompoop around, and so they settled for a NEEDLEFISH from Blog's aquarium instead.
"O!"
"OLD OLIVE OIL!"
"P!"

"PEPPER!" cried the witch, and from her apron she took a bag of the hottest pepper. She dumped the pepper into the soup, and the cauldron started to shake. The soup dribbled into the flames. Zack pulled his sweater up over his nose.

"Q!" called Gurgla.

"Qui…Quo…Quack…" For a moment they were stumped.

"QUESTION MARK!" shouted Blog, and drew a perfect question mark in the bubbling liquid.

"What a clever little boy!" exclaimed the witch. She thought that Blog might become a famous witch doctor one day.

"R and S!" whined hungry Gurgla. The fumes were wicked. Zack rubbed his eyes.

"Rats and snakes would be perfect," he snickered. The witch, as if she had heard him, reached into another jar and pulled out something slimy and disgusting.

"Pickled RATS coming up!" she hissed. "And pickled SNAKES on the double!"

There was a splash, and Blog stirred the pot.

"T, U, V!" Gurgla cried, and tossed her plastic TARANTULA into the boiling pot. The only U thing they could think of was their mother's UKULELE. It melted like a Popsicle.

"V!" cried Gurgla.

The VAMPIRE TEETH Blog had been saving for show-and-tell soon bubbled in the broth.

"Only four letters to go!" yelled Gurgla. "W, X, Y, and Z!"

Zack wondered if they would drink it or eat it with a spoon. The old witch had gone inside to fetch some dishes.

"W, as in WORMS," said Blog, and collected some crawling things from the ground. He stirred the soup very gently now so as not to spoil the delicate flavor. For the letter X they crossed two chicken bones, stuck them together with a ball of earwax…and ta-da! into the pot they went. But darn, the letter Y was giving them serious trouble. They were stuck!

"Wee, Wye, Woe, Wum…" Gurgla and Blog rattled their brains, but in vain because they were too hungry to think.

Zack knew of many things beginning with Y, like yolk, yeast, or yogurt, and he was very tempted to give them a hint. Just then the witch rushed out of the hut waving a bottle in her hand.

"For the letter Y," she cried, "we'll add a little WINE!" She emptied the bottle into the pot, and the soup was almost done.

Gurgla was about to call the last letter of the alphabet, when suddenly something stirred in the bushes.

"Hi!" said Zack as he stepped into the clearing. He was an excellent speller. "I don't mean to interrupt, but I think you've made a mistake. Wine doesn't begin with the letter Y; it just sounds like it. It begins with the letter doub—" But the witch didn't let him finish.

"Snooping around, aren't we?" croaked the old hag. "Smarty-pants!"

Gurgla and Blog recognized him right away. "That's Zack from our school, Mom!" squealed the twins.

"ZACK?" The witch blinked. She made an awful grin, showing her only tooth. "What a pretty name Zack is. Doesn't it begin with the letter Z?"

"It does, Mother," cried the twins. "It does!"

At that moment, Zack realized what a terrible mistake HE had just made.

"Zack," whined the witch, "come and help us stir the pot." She pinched his cheek. "A little skinny, aren't we?"

In a flash, Zack saw the danger he was in. He was the last ingredient in their alphabet soup!

"Never!" he yelled, and he ran into the woods. Why didn't his parents call him Bob? Or Eddie? He ran fast.

But Gurgla and Blog opened the garage door. Inside was a large broom. They sat on it, mother in front, and *swooooosh!* they were in the air.

"Zack for Z and Z for Zack!" they screamed. They were as hungry as a horse, and they were after him.

Zack climbed into the highest tree.

"Zack for Z and Z for Zack!" they screamed again, and parked the broom under the tree. They climbed after him. First the witch, then Gurgla, then Blog.

"Zack," shrieked the witch, "how about a ride on a broom!"

"You'll never get me!" shouted Zack. He climbed higher and higher. But the witch caught up with him, and he could feel her claws pulling on his sneakers. His sneakers were untied and slipped right off.

"Blast!" cried the witch, and she grabbed his pants. Her claws were like iron hooks.

"I've got him!" she cried. "I've got him good!" She gave a powerful tug and *pop!* the button on Zack's pants snapped and bonked the witch square on the head.

"Aieeeee!" screamed the witch as she tumbled to the ground. She landed with a *thwack*, squashing the twins under her. In her grubby hands she had an empty pair of blue jeans.

"Oh, rats!" hissed the witch. She looked up. In the top of the tree Zack was swaying in the evening breeze. All of a sudden Gurgla and Blog started to shout.

"Zipper for Z and Z for Zipper!" they chanted, waving Zack's pants like a banner.

"Look Mom!" cried Gurgla. "A Zipper!"

The witch didn't seem to understand.

"For Z!" shouted Blog.

"Ah!" cried the witch. "ZIPPER for Z!" She started up the broom and swoosh, they were back at the hut.

"He was too skinny anyway," said the witch, and they threw Zack's blue jeans into the cauldron to boil. At long last, the alphabet soup was done.

When they had gone, Zack climbed down from the tree, and although he was still very curious, he was also very cold. Barefoot and without any pants on, he ran to the village and jumped in his bed.

And that was just too bad, because back at the hut, the fun was just beginning. Gurgla and Blog were having company for dinner.

Their cousins, the five wickedest trolls you have ever seen, were gobbling up the alphabet soup, zipper and all, and they loved it. They slurped and smacked and when they had licked the cauldron clean, the cousins begged for the recipe.

The witch whispered something into their dirty ears and the next morning…

When Miss Smith came into the classroom, five new students were sitting in the front row, eager to learn the alphabet.

"Good morning Miss Smith!" said the class.

"Good morning, children," said Miss Smith, and being the good sport that she was, she took out her nail scissors and went to work.

Zack was unusually quiet that day.